Mac the Rabbit

About Mossburn...

At Mossburn Animal Centre in Scotland, UK we rescue and shelter misused, abused, unwanted and neglected animals, and provide therapeutic work placements for children and adults with problems. Our aim is to enhance the lives of both animals and people through our animal rescue work. Animal shelters play a vital role in ensuring the happiness and well-being of animals and in educating prospective pet owners in the care of their animal.

Mossburn Animal Centre was originally set up in 1987 to provide help for misused, abused, unwanted and neglected horses and ponies as well as young people with physical and mental problems. This original remit was later widened, and we now care for all domestic animals except cats, dogs and donkeys which have their own specific charities. In addition we nurse and rehabilitate wildlife.

Mossburn Animal Centre is run entirely on goodwill donations from our visitors, friends and animal fosterers. We hope that you will browse our web site and help the animals you meet there by becoming a Friend of Mossburn or an Animal Fosterer, and join in with the fun of naming some of our new arrivals!

We welcome visitors on the ground as well as on the Web and hope that we will have the opportunity to welcome you to Mossburn so that you can see the value of our animal rescue work and our shelter provision first hand.

Registered Charity Number SCO 21652
Mossburn Animal Centre, Hightae,
Lockerbie, Dumfries and Galloway, Scotland.
Tel: 01387 811288 Fax: 01387 810012
web: www.mossburn.org
email: mossburnanimalcentre2@hotmail.com

Mac
the
Rabbit

by Hugh McMillan

illustrated by Chris White

The King's England Press

2003

ISBN 1 872438 92 X

Mac the Rabbit is typeset in 12pt Times New Roman by the
King's England Press and published by

The King's England Press
Cambertown House
Commercial Road
Goldthorpe
ROTHERHAM S63 9BL

PRINTED AND BOUND IN GREAT BRITAIN BY
JOHN BRAILSFORD PRINT
RAWMARSH HILL
PARKGATE
ROTHERHAM

Chapter 1

'SICK OF COUNTIN BLADES OF GRASS
SICK OF SITTIN ON HIS TAIL
MAC CUT LOOSE, HIT THE TRAIL'
(from 'Mac' by 'Rabbit Rage',
lyrics © Bunnytone Records, 2001)

Mac the Rabbit looked up, saw the sun sinking a fiery red behind Criffel. It was a good time of day for rabbits, when they would all come out of their burrows to enjoy the last sunlight on their fur and catch up with all the gossip. Mac was different from the others. He had reached a difficult age. Nothing pleased him. He chewed the grass in an insolent manner, leaning against the dyke with his eyes half shut. He stayed out late, playing chicken with the cars on the main road. He stole carrots and played guitar for a group called 'Rabbit Rage'. He hung out with the wrong rabbits. He wore a grunge jacket made from an old potato sack. He was a rabbit without a cause. For all these reasons, Mac didn't enjoy the end of the day when the other rabbits were winding down. The end of *his* day was filled with a great dissatisfaction. Most of all, when he wasn't thinking of cool things to say in a bored way, he looked with a great longing out at the world beyond the edges of the four fields, at the strange shaped hills, the trees marching like soldiers towards the horizon and sometimes, when it was very bright and clear and there was no mist, at the distant sea itself.

There are people who think that rabbits can't be interested in rock music, games or gossip. They think they just sit about munching the grass, their heads empty as clouds, or twitching their noses in a cute way and running off. Or they think like a vet or biology teacher might, that rabbits are unusual in a way, mostly because they digest their food in a way you wouldn't tell your granny. What's wrong with these people? Time they wised up, read some books, or watched some films, or even bought Rabbit Rage's new CD:

'YOU THINK WE'RE GRASS CHEWERS
YOU THINK WE'RE ALL LOSERS,
BUT HERE'S SOMETHING FOR YOU TO STEW,
THERE'S MORE OF US THAN YOU.'

(from 'Kill the Bunny' by Rabbit Rage, available from all good record outlets)

The problem with human beings is that they think they're the whole cheese and that rabbits, like every other species of animal, are there to entertain them, or look cute, or welcome them home. Next time they look at a rabbit, they should try and think what *it*'s feeling.

Mac had been taught, by his Great-Great-Grandfather Sasha, of the great part rabbits have played through history. Like all the young ones at one time or another, he'd squatted on the cosy leaf-lined floor of Sasha's study that was lined with books and marble statues of all the good and wise and famous rabbits of the past, and listened to the old rabbit tell tales of the great ones, like the warrior Attila the Hutch, spies like Mata Hare, film stars like Warren Beattie and Dennis Hopper and Carrot O'Hara.*

* As well as gangsters like Bunny Corleone, and the tyrant most rabbits don't want to talk about, Bunnyto Mussolini.

6

It was the stories of the explorers he'd liked best, the rabbits who'd travelled and first set their big back feet on foreign lands, first felt the Africa winds on their whiskers or the cold north wind. Like Angora Vespucci, the first rabbit to spot America.

"Rabbits," Sasha had said one day, "have been in this country for 2000 years." He'd tapped his stick on the floor for emphasis. "When Julius Caesar first sailed here, he was driven out by a tough force of rabbits. He …. Yes?" Mac had tentatively raised a paw. "I thought," said Mac nervously, "Well, I'd heard that … read actually that …" He could feel Sasha's gaze on his face. "Well, I'd heard" said Mac all in one brave breath, "that they thought rabbits were food, not soldiers." There had been a long silence. "Mac," said Sasha at last, in a patient way, "would you kindly look out the window?" Mac had done so, stretching his long back legs to look at the field outside. "How many rabbits do you see?" Sasha had asked. Mac had looked as carefully as he could, "'Bout 60 or 70," he'd answered. Sasha had stared at him then at the rest of the class before turning back. "And how many Romans?" Mac had taken the point. Rabbits ruled.

As time went on, however, Mac had become restless. It seemed that rabbits nowadays had settled for an easy life, an "I'm all right Jackrabbit" type of existence. No-one even wondered what was going on on the other side of the dyke, never mind at the other end of the world. Mac got bored with the constant round of birthdays, weddings and funerals of those rabbits killed on the A701. He wanted to see more of the world, enjoy what it had to offer. Live off the fat of the land for a while. One night he turned to some of his brothers and said, "Aren't you curious about what's going on right at this moment in Cairo? Don't you ever wonder where all these miles of road go? Where all these walls end up. What happens

…" Mac pointed to the horizon, "if you go over that line? Do you fall off the end?" But all his family had done was shrugged and carried on eating, although one or two of the younger ones had, behind Mac's back, tapped their front paws against the side of their heads, indicating he was a loony.

The next morning, when everyone was asleep, Mac crept round the burrow, collecting his most valuable possessions and putting them in a little knapsack. He took his large piece of string, the compass his grandfather had given him, and the old bag, torn into scraps, on which he'd intended to write a youth masterpiece in the style of 'On the Road' by his hero, Jack Kerrouabbit. He meant to keep a diary of his travels, write some lyrics. Before he left, he scribbled a small note:

GONE TO SEE THE WORLD DON'T WAIT UP

After that, he silently lifted the latch and was gone, into the cold light of day.

Chapter 2

'IT'S THE MORNING,
HOPE IT'S DAWNING
ONE A NEW DAY, A NEW HIGHWAY.'
(from 'Mac' by 'Rabbit Rage')

Mac walked for some hours across fields not too different from his own, with the air full of the scent of hawthorn and new grass. It was a beautiful day and the sun was warm, even when it was barely daylight. He stopped to pick up a little piece of wood and used it to swish the ends of weeds as he walked along. He felt like a great rabbit, from the pages of history. He set off towards the sea. Occasionally, he would look at his grandfather's compass, just for fun, as the hands had fallen off some years before. Time passed, and the sun came overhead then passed him and began to sink in the sky. Mac clambered through a mossy gap in a dyke at last and found himself at the foot of a hill ringed by tall fir trees.

He stopped for a moment. Trees were not his natural home, but if he climbed to the top of the hill what views might he have? What stories might he be able to tell the other rabbits? What songs could he write?

He began to trudge resolutely through the first of the trees. The smell was different here, stronger. His nose twitched. As he went on, the trees became more dense, thicker and the light began to disappear altogether. Strange fluttering and scattering noises came from either side. Mac shivered and peered deeper into the gathering gloom. Rabbits' eyes were good in the dark but Mac was not used to forests and the noises scared him. He stopped, glanced around him. All he could make out was the lifting of leaves and all he could hear was the loud whisper of branches far above his head. He crept forward, pressed himself against the back of a tree. The wind had risen, moaning softly through the wood like an animal in pain. The shadows were swaying on the ground like monsters. Suddenly he felt scared about the adventure and thought about the warmth of the burrow, the hot breath, the portraits of his white furred grandfathers nailed on the walls; the world he had thought so boring. Then, with a little surge of bravery, he got out his notebook and with some difficulty, because it was so dark, wrote:

ON THE ROAD - DAY ONE: KICKIN'!

Then he pulled himself together, swallowed, shouldered his knapsack and made to stride off, but, only a few yards further on, he was shocked to the core by an ear-splitting boom that made the leaves, even the ground itself, shake. Birds rose in a cloud, screaming. Mac couldn't imagine what was going on. He cowered again against the bark of a tree, his ears ringing. Straining, he could make out muffled sounds, wood breaking as if some chase was on. He looked back but there was no safety behind him, not for many miles, only darkness and shapes. All the bravery left him like the puff from a balloon. He would have swapped places with one of his stupid brothers now alright, and be back home making small snoring noises and wagging his feet as he dreamed of the next day. There was a sudden quiet.

Things went quiet then, and after a minute, Mac extended one big ear round the side of the tree, then his nose. There was a mixture of smells, some bad some good. He could smell humans, like the ones who'd run his Uncle Roderick down and tossed his body over the wall like rubbish. Mac hadn't met many humans - they travelled down the grey tube beyond the wall and sometimes came into the fields to worry the sheep. They were trouble but they didn't mix too much with rabbits - probably scared. That's why they travelled so quickly round the countryside in armoured cars. But Mac knew they were dangerous when roused and here in the wood he smelled fear and death.

He stuck his head further out, set his whiskers to the wind. There wasn't a living being, he thought, who could surprise a rabbit. He gingerly moved round the tree and in a sudden heart-stopping moment found himself staring into two huge eyes. He got such a fright he dropped his stick and was about to run, when he heard a small voice. "Help," it said, in a most miserable and pathetic way.

Mac's heart was beating like an engine and he could sense the danger - the human danger - coming closer but he hissed, "Run, whoever you are. Follow me and don't stop running. Keep the wind at your back." And he set off at top speed, west along the crown of the hill, dodging and swerving through the undergrowth, with this creature keeping pace behind in a kind of lolloping gambolling stride. Mac looked round once but could only see knees.

They ran for some time, to the very edge of the wood. By now the day was nearly over, but there was still a kind of half light through the least dense trees. Mac slid to a halt and so did his companion. Breathing hard, Mac took his first real look at the creature. It was long legged, like on stilts, spotted brown and white, with a wet black nose not unlike his own. "Who are you?" Mac asked. "Fern," came the reply. "And what kind of thing are you?" "Deer," said the exhausted animal, "small deer," and then she sank down in a deep sleep.

Mac dozed too, but spent most of the night on the alert, pacing around the folded fawn with its rank smell of fear. Mac could not detect any danger and as the night progressed, he became very proud. He had already had a great adventure. At first light he took out his notebook and wrote:

HELPED SMALL DEER: YO!

Then he fell asleep in a hollow that smelled of pine and bluebells.

His friend was up first, poking him gently with a hoof. Mac focused sleepily on the deer. "Are you a kind of horse?" he asked. Fern laughed. "No. We graze like you, but we live in the woods, the hills. We are very shy, hurt no-one but humans sometimes hate us."

"Why?" asked Mac. "I can't understand them. They seem to think they own the place. Why do they hate you?"

"They kill us for fun," said Fern.

Mac shivered. "Not even to eat?" That idea was ridiculous enough.

"For fun."

Mac shook his head. "Were they shooting at you?"

"My family," said the fawn. "I don't know where they are now. Maybe they're ..." She looked miserable again. Mac nudged her. Her skin was soft and smooth, not furred like Mac's.

"Never mind," he said gently. "We'll stick together, you and I. I was on an adventure, you see, but now I have no idea where I am."

"Me neither," said Fern.

"Well come on," said Mac, more cheerfully than he felt. "We'll find safety somewhere." And they set off to find the end of the wood.

Chapter Three

'ANIMALS FALLING
ADVENTURE CALLING -
TIME FOR MAC TO MOVE!
(from 'Mac' by Rabbit Rage)

Fern and Mac continued to travel through the wood till at last they came to a wide river. The water was swollen with recent rain and was fast moving. Mac looked at it and the spindly legs of the fawn. "Don't fancy that," he said. Fern shook her head. "Wonder if there's a bridge." They walked upstream for a while through ancient oak trees. Occasionally they heard the rustle of small animals in the undergrowth but they didn't see anyone. A considerable time passed and still there was no sign of a crossing. Suddenly Mac stopped dead. He looked round at his friend; her nose was twitching. "Humans," said Mac, "talking". Fern nodded. Normally the animals would have avoided contact with humans at all costs, but these voices were quite young. In Mac's experience most young people, though not all, mean to be kinder than grown-ups. And where there are humans there would be tracks, roads, bridges. Great builders, men, all in a headlong rush somewhere or other. They approached very cautiously, peered through wide leaves. There were two young boys, standing below a rope swing. They were using a catapult.

"What's that?" whispered Fern.

"Weapon," grunted Mac. "Throws stones at high speed. Nasty."

The animals watched as one of the boys, a tall skinny youth with glasses, picked up a stone and fitted it into the pouch of the catapult. He took aim and let fly. The stone crashed into the branches and a bird took off, squawking with fear.

"Well," said Fern angrily. "That's humans for you."

Mac's whiskers bristled. He felt the blood of his hero rabbit ancestors stir in his veins. The boy had taken another stone and, urged on by his friend, was aiming at the top of another tree. "Come on," he said, "You'll get it this time."

Mac had heard enough. He strode through the branches and approached the boys from behind. The boy continued to adjust his aim. "Ahem," coughed Mac, tapping his foot on the floor. The boys whirled round in surprise and looked at thin air, then down to where Mac stood. The smaller boy whooped. "Yes," he cried, "a real target!" The bigger one quickly adjusted the catapult, aiming it straight at Mac's head.

The rabbit didn't panic but instead said, in a loud clear voice, "IF YOU HIT ME WITH THAT, FOUR EYES, YOU'LL BE REALLY SORRY."

Both boys went white and their mouths fell open. There was a moment's pause then, dropping the catapult on the ground, both turned and ran. Mac picked up the catapult and strolled back to his friend. He opened up his bundle, took out his notebook, licked his pencil and carefully wrote down
RABBIT RESPECT!

"That's another thing about humans," said Mac as they were following the boys' trail. "They think that because animals keep themselves to themselves, that they're more stupid than them."

The trail was easy to follow, and after a few minutes they saw, to their satisfaction, a small bridge. They crossed it, then, keeping away from the right of two tracks which led to some cottages, they carried on through trees which began gradually to thin. At last they came to a meadow. Mac could feel the sun properly again. This was more his kind of country. They stopped to eat a little, Fern keeping close to the tree-line. "I wonder where we are," she said. Mac shook his head. "The world is endless," he said. "It is a cool and wild place." He was rather proud of that and would have written it down in his notebook if he hadn't been so hungry.

After a while, a strange sound came to their ears, more urgent than a rippling stream, more like a cough but sadder. More adventure, thought Mac, there's no end to it. They crept down the fringe of the trees to a low hedge, then drew back. Mac nodded grimly. "Another small human," he whispered. Mac squirmed forward and squinted through the undergrowth. A girl sat on the grass weeping. Mac had never seen anyone crying before - humans are the only ones who cry, readers, and you can draw your own conclusions from that - but it was obvious that the girl was very sad. She was small, not even quarter grown, far younger than the boys in the wood. She was wearing a dress with wood violets on it and had plaited hair, yellow as corn.

"Come on," whispered Fern, "Let's go." Mac thought for a moment. You will know by now that Mac was no ordinary animal, if any animal can be said to be ordinary. Instead of turning tail, he crept through the bushes till he was sitting upright next to the girl. She looked up and saw him and stopped weeping out of sheer surprise. Mac was making a habit of surprising people, and still does to this day, even when he's not on tour. "What's wrong?" he said.

A word should be said here about the language of animals, because many of you reading this book will be thinking *you*'ve never heard a rabbit talk, or a dog, or a cat, or a hamster (you can be pleased about that - hamsters are so boring, even worse than gerbils, all they care about is nuts and seeing how far they can climb up the curtains before they fall on their heads) but there is more to talking than opening your mouth and all of you will have known people who would swear that they knew exactly what their pet meant to say to them. Animals find their way of saying things to each other and to us, even though mostly we're not worth talking to. It helps to be young, when you've not quite made up your mind that you're sure about everything and you still believe that improbable, or even impossible, things can happen if you're lucky enough.

The little girl gaped at Mac then looked round, as if she was trying to see someone playing tricks on her.

"No," said Mac quietly, "It was me. I am a rabbit on the road."

The girl shuffled closer to Mac and he allowed her to put one grubby hand on his head. "Well I never," she said.

"Hello, Never," said Mac, "I am Mac and over there behind that hedge is Fern the Fawn. She is a bit more timid than I am but it is not her fault. I am used to public adoration cos I'm in a rock band called Rabbit Rage. You've heard of them, of course?"

The girl shook her head and Mac, put out a bit, furiously cleaned his whiskers. "You are sad," he said, somewhat huffily.

"Why?"

"I'm sad about Shanghai."

Mac thought back to his geography lessons with Sasha.

"Isn't that a large coastal city in China, with a serious earthquake problem?"

"No," she said smiling, "it's a Vietnamese pot bellied pig."

Fern had crept out and was eyeing the girl suspiciously. "A what?" she asked. The girl's eyes widened.

"Pig," said Mac. Mac knew what pigs were. He'd met a pig once and they'd had an argument underneath a thorn bush about who were the best, pigs or rabbits. When Mac had started to talk about the famous rabbits, the pig had started droning on about how his ancestors used to live wild in the forests and fight knights in armour who were trying to hunt them. "We were wild boars," the pig had said, snootily. Not wild any more, Mac had thought, but still bores.

"A Vietnamese pot bellied pig," the girl had repeated. "They come from far away and they're kept as pets by some people to show off, then they can't look after them properly cos they need a lot of money and a lot of attention and that's what's happened to Shanghai." The girl had begun to sob again.

"Steady, Never," Mac said kindly. "Tell us the whole story."

It turned out that someone called Smythe, a rich human, had bought the old house next door to Morgan's, as a holiday house and had bought the pig to live in the garden so he could show it off at parties. "But Smythe's never there now and there's only a caretaker who lives there and never talked to Shanghai who never comes out of his shed anymore and I don't think he feeds him properly. Pot bellied pigs need a diet rich in protein and nutrients, you know."

"Don't we all," muttered Fern, rubbing her stomach.

"Is the house near?" asked Mac.

Morgan nodded. "Just down that drive." She pointed to a red tiled roof beyond a tall hedge. Mac immediately began to stride off, Fern running to catch up. "Now come on, Mac," she said, "We've had enough adventures for one day. Let's not get into anything hasty." In the distance they heard a dog barking. Fern stiffened. "They've got a big black dog tied up," said the girl breathlessly, "Shanghai's scared of it."

They reached the long hedge that bounded the garden of the house. A human was shouting in the distance. "I have to go in now for tea," she said, "but I'll sneak out after dark."

"Meet us here," said Mac.

Following the hedge they came to some fir trees. Fern ate and settled down. "I'm so sleepy," she groaned.

"Wait here," said Mac, "I'm going to see what's going on. What we rabbits call a reconnaissance mission." Mac flattened himself against the hedge and carefully edged along it. Behind the hedge he could see a tall wire mesh fence, probably about twelve feet high. Through the fence was a carefully laid out garden. The fence skirted south round a pond, then, at the widest part of the pond it stopped, starting again at the furthest side. Here he had a clearer view of the garden. A large black dog, tethered to a long chain, was standing in the middle of the lawn. Behind him to the left was a squat black shed that Mac supposed was Shanghai's home. To the right was a little hut, probably for gardening tools, and the side of a big house. He moved closer to the pond, trying to measure how wide and deep it was.

"Forget it," said a voice. Mac turned round to be faced with another rabbit, slightly smaller than himself, but standing cockily on two legs squinting at him. "Looks great, don't it?" The rabbit was chewing, but smiling in a lazy, friendly way.

"What?" asked Mac, puzzled.

21

"Oh, don't mess. Don't pretend you wasn't looking at it - the garden, dummy. The best bit of eating this side of the Atlantic. Would be in there guzzling away, chewing the fat myself, if it wasn't for the fence, the alarm bells, the searchlights, the pond, and that big four-legged thing with the eight rows of teeth."

"Ah," said Mac and looked again. Right enough the lawn was a beautiful shade of emerald green and there were neat rows of plants and vegetables in a big kitchen garden nearer the house.

"Rabbit could go mad looking at that kind of thing," muttered the other. Then he looked at Mac again. "You from these parts?"

Mac gestured vaguely. "Over the big hill," he said.

"Wow. Some trip. I'm Yank, by the way." He extended a paw.

"Mac," said Mac, shaking it.

"And these are Pongo, Skipper, Brains, Sparks, Windy and Dandy," said Yank, introducing a group of rabbits who had just emerged from the undergrowth.

"Hi," said Mac.

"Nice to see you, old man," said Pongo, slapping him on the back. The others took their turn to shake paws. "This dude's been casing the joint," said Yank. The others laughed.

"Actually," said Mac, "I was thinking of trying to rescue the pig that lives there."

"A PIG?" repeated Pongo. The others were laughing.

"Yeah," said Yank, "there's an elephant there, too."

"And a gorilla," laughed Skipper.

"And an aardvark," said Brains. The others stared at him. "An earth pig that translates, by the way, in case you were ignorant of the language of the ..."

"Cripes," said Windy, "Where do you get all the rubbish from?"

"The London School of Ecorabbits, actually," muttered Brains, sulkily.

"No," said Mac, cutting through the growing noise. "I'm serious. I'm helping a little girl called Never. There's a Vietnamese pot bellied pig being kept against its will in there."

"Ah," said Brains. "Vietnam. That takes me back to …"

"Ah, put a cake in it," said Yank. "Yeah, we've seen the girl. Not a bad little thing. Tried to talk to us once or twice … but you know, gotta play safe these days." The others nodded, including Mac. "I'm going to help her if I can," said Mac. "I'm on the road, you see."

Yank raised his eyebrows. "An adventure, eh boys? Bin a bit boring round here lately, wanna lend a hand?" They thought for a while, rubbing their chins. "Hey," said Pongo at last, "Don't I know you? Aren't you in a band?"

Chapter 4

'MEANING IN LIFE
TROUBLE AND STRIFE
A RABBIT'S GOTTA LIVE'
(from 'Rabbit Riot')

A Council of Rabbits is a very rare thing, happening only in times of emergency. Rabbits are naturally friendly to each other, and very good neighbours, but hardly ever meet in great numbers. So you can imagine why the little girl called Never was so surprised when, led by Mac the Rabbit and Fern, she came to a clearing in the wood later that night and found herself standing behind a great old three-legged table surrounded by about 800 rabbits, all talking at once.

"Quiet!" Yank was shouting, "QUIET!" The noise got a bit less. "The idea," Yank said to the crowd, "is that our friend here, Mac, from over the hills, wants our help to get into the Smythe Place." There was a lot of muttering at this, some snorts of disbelief. "To," continued Yank, "help a pig." There was an outbreak of laughter at this and a few angry shouts. Some rabbit near the front was booing. "No, listen," yelled Yank, but the noise was too great and some of the rabbits at the back had started to leave. Mac jumped to the front and with the loud voice he reserved for getting his own way, shouted, "Won't you listen? Where I come from, strangers are treated with politeness." This wasn't true at all, but it stopped some of the rabbits from shouting and a few others shuffled back into place. One, dressed in a ripped black T-shirt, even shouted "Yo! Rabbit Rage!"

Mac took his chance. "You don't care about pigs, and to be honest I don't know if I do either. The only one I every met was a real big head. But we know rabbits, don't we?" There was much nodding of heads. "We know rabbits who have disappeared?" There was a murmuring in the crowd. "Rabbits who have been run down?" Some of the crowd bowed their heads. "Rabbits" - here Mac's voice broke a little - "rabbits who are still dying of the great poison?" There were some angry cries of "Yes!"

"Every time," said Mac, more quietly, "every time we do nothing, every time we turn our back, every time we go about our business and forget the suffering of others, every time we do that, we convince the humans that we are only fit for food, or pests, or - pets!" He spat the last word out. The crowd were now listening eagerly to Mac's every word. He heard Yank muttering, "Way to go, Mac!"

"I don't know very much," said Mac, increasing the sound of his voice again, "I'm only a rabbit, though actually I'm quite talented musically." (Here he played a little bit of air guitar.) "But I know that though we are small, our hearts are huge!" There was a cheer from the crowd. "And I know this, too … that for evil to triumph, it is only necessary for good rabbits to do nothing. Now! Who's going to help us?" There was a roar of approval from the crowd. The little girl and Fern stood beaming and clapping. Mac had won the day.

Decisions were quickly made. A small team of the fittest rabbits was formed under the command of Mac and Yank. The Rabbit Response Squad, Brains called it. With Morgan's help, a sketch map was drawn in Mac's notebook. This is it:

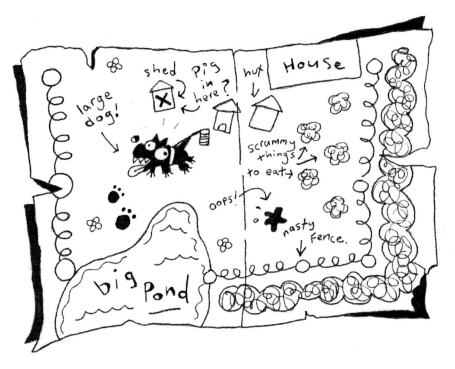

Later that night, the RRS and Fern and Morgan sat to work out a plan. It wasn't easy. "Obviously," said Brains, "we can burrow under the wire."

Yank nodded. "But we can't get a pig out through a burrow."

"And the moment we set foot in the garden the dog will get us," said Pongo, "or start barking and wake up the guard."

"Yes," said Mac, "the dog is the key. Put the dog out of action and the rest might be possible."

"Why don't you go and make him a speech?" said Windy. "It works with rabbits." Mac examined the other rabbit for signs of sarcasm, but there didn't seem to be any.

"The dog's a trained killer," said Yank, "It'd have your neck before you cleared your throat."

They all thought for a while. "Does it sleep in its kennel at night?" asked Mac.

"Think so," said Skipper. "It would be stupid not to. It still gets very cold here at night."

"Does the kennel have a door?"

Yank nodded. "Man shuts it up sometimes when he's in the garden. Got a bolt on the outside I think."

"So," said Brains, "You're thinking we could lock it in its kennel?"

"Trouble is," said Mac, "As soon as we got into the garden, he'd smell us. We couldn't get there fast enough. It's about a hundred feet from the fence to the kennel. I don't know how fast a hopper you are …?" Yank was shaking his head. "There has to be another way," said Mac quietly, "There has to be."

"And what about the guard?" said Fern. "What do we know about him?"

"Big," said Pongo. "Fat, likes his grub, but BIG. Wouldn't like to see him in action."

Windy shook his head. "Sounds like Mission Impossible," he said.

"Well," said Mac, picking up his bundle. "What have we got that'll help us?" He took out his store. "Big bit of string. A catapult, paper and a broken compass. Not much, eh? What have you got?"

"Just what we stand up in," laughed Yank, "Though Dandy here's got some coat hangers." The rabbit called Dandy blushed. "Fell off the back of a lorry," he muttered.

"Coat hangers," said Mac, looking at the tall trees that overlooked the garden. "How's your head for heights?"

Chapter 5

'NO MORE FACTIONS
NOW'S TIME FOR ACTION
RABBIT, WAY TO GO!'
(from 'The Battle of Shanghai')

So, how could a group of rabbits rescue a Vietnamese pot bellied pig from a well guarded area with a deep pond, high security fences, searchlights, a mad dog and a guard, using

A piece of string

Two coat hangers

A catapult

A broken compass

Paper

Other things lying about?

Amazing though it seems, Mac thought of two plans. One of these, that he decided to try, is written about next. The other, which he thought was just as likely to work, or not to work, remains a secret. But if any reader thinks they're as clever as Mac the Rabbit and the Rabbit Response Force and can come up with an alternative plan, they should write it down and send it to the address at the end of the book, where Mac the Rabbit now lives. He has a prize which he'll give to the answer nearest his Plan B. More of that at the end, however.

The rabbits, Fern and the little girl spent the next day preparing to put Mac's daring plan into action. In the late afternoon, Mac held another planning meeting in the wood. He called it his 'dress rehearsal'. The rabbits quickly gathered round a tree on which Mac had pinned another sheet of his paper. "OK, chaps, settle down," said Pongo, "C.O. wants to talk to you." There was an excited hush. Mac straightened his whiskers then pointed with a twig at the sketch map on the tree. "OK, lads, it's important we know this plan like the back of our paws, and that each and every rabbit, deer and girl know their jobs. Timing is vital here. We are all part of a well oiled machine." The others nodded gravely. Brains adjusted his glasses.

"Phase One," said Mac, striking his twig at the part of the picture that showed the Big House. The girl cleared her throat. "I get up really early and deliver this note through the letter box of the house." She held up a grubby piece of paper from Mac's notebook. It read:

BIG OFER IN TOWN TONITE

FREE PIZAS

HALF SEVEN IN PIZA PLACE

HI STREET

There was a picture drawn at the bottom and coloured in by the girl. It looked like a stagnant puddle to Mac but Morgan said it looked exactly like a pizza. None of the rabbits knew what a pizza was so they weren't going to argue. When the rabbits saw the note they burst into applause. "Very clever indeed," muttered Brains in admiration.

Mac continued. "Phase Two," he announced. Fern stood forward. "Deer and rabbit Undercover Squad make way using cover round boundary fence to recovery area Z." Mac tapped a large Z on the map, at a position beyond the fence to the left of the big house. "Then they dig two tunnels and wait." She stood back, flushed and smiling.

"Phase Three," said Mac. Pongo saluted smartly. "Rabbit Response Force Tree Climbing Section go up tall tree

Y" - Mac indicated the letter Y on the map with his stick - "led by C.O.s and carrying a large piece of string and small rock. SAH!" He clicked his back legs together and stepped back.

"Phase Four." "Phrase Four," said Sparks, "Field Engineers take coat hangers and catapult to base of tree Y and tie to large piece of string dangling there."

"Five," said Mac, pleased at the well-drilled way things were going. "Tree Climbing Unit secure coat hangers and catapult in tree base," barked Pongo.

"Phase Six." Yank strolled forward, a small stick dangling from the side of his mouth. "After greedy guts goes for the pizza, we fire the catapult and send the string, tied to the rock, winging all the way to Point Z|."

"Seven." "Undercover Squad," said Windy, "tie end of string to bottom of fence making secure line from tree base."

Mac nodded. "Phase Nine," he said, and supplied the answer himself. "Commandos descend rapidly and silently from tree top using coat hangers and string to point above kennel, then free-fall to ground, shutting kennel door before Devil Dog has woken up. Phase Ten."

"Special Boat Squadron," said Skipper, "paddle across pond on three-legged table, upturned."

"And Eleven." "Commandos release pig before man comes home angry at being conned out of piza. Pig is evacuated by Special Boat Squadron."

"Twelve," said Mac, "Commandos make for recovery point Z and use escape tunnels." There was a tense silence. "Game over," said Yank.

They ran through the plans a couple more times, made an equipment check, then tried to settle down for the night. Morgan went home, excitedly clutching her note. Few of the rabbits could sleep. Mac looked up at the stars, his paws folded behind his head. Somewhere, everywhere, these stars were shining down on all the animals in the world. He looked round at his fellow rabbits. How many of them would make it through tomorrow? A lump began in his throat. Yank was whistling softly, a tune he didn't recognise. "What's that?" he whispered. Yank began to sing in a soft, sweet voice that didn't fit his appearance at all:

> "Don't sit under the apple tree
> with any bunny but me,
> any bunny but me,
> any bunny but me.
> Don't sit under the apple tree
> with any bunny but me
> Till I come marching home."

There was a deep quiet, but then Fern started singing 'Deer Meet Again' and there was a confusion about the spelling, and the spell was broken and Mac didn't even get the chance to sing his new composition 'The Battle of Shanghai'. Never mind, he thought, it would be heard in the months and years to come wherever rabbits gathered together to discuss famous deeds. They'd better give him royalties, mind you.

Chapter 6

'NERVES LIKE FIRE
BLOOD AND FIRE
RABBITS GO TO WAR!'
(from 'The Battle of Shanghai')

Day dawned, crisp and cold. The rabbits were up at first light, limbering and loosening up, getting the cold out of their limbs, and cleaning and preparing the equipment. They assembled in their squads:

Tree Climbing Unit - Mac, Yank and Pongo
Special Operations Squad - Sparks and Brains
Undercover Squad - Fern and Windy
Special Boat Squadron - Skipper and Dandy

The girl arrived to say, breathlessly, that she'd delivered the note. In mid-morning, Fern and Windy set out, cautiously keeping to cover, on their long journey round the fence.

The rest of the day passed painfully slowly. At last the sun changed sides, and morning turned into afternoon, then late afternoon. Mac, Yank and Pongo stood underneath the giant fir tree. "Well, Mac," smiled Yank. "How's your tree-climbing?"

"Don't know," said Mac, "Ask me after this one; it's my first." He wound the string round his waist and tied the end to his wrist. The rabbits laughed, slapped each other on the back and shook paws. Brains and Sparks saluted smartly. "Good luck, sir. Break a leg." "Bring back the bacon!" laughed the girl.

Mac swallowed, looked up at the height of the tree. "OK, lads?" The other two nodded, and Mac began to slowly climb the tree.

Note on Tree Climbing Rabbits: How many people do you think have climbed up a great big tree for a laugh, or to pick apples, or to watch sycamore helicopters spin to the earth, and found a rabbit at the top already? The answer to that question, I'll bet, is no-one. This tells you more about the terrible task facing Pongo, Mac and Yank than any description I could give you about that awful climb itself. Rabbits do not climb trees. They do not have the physical make up. They do not have suction pads, or ice-axes, or those really strong helmets with cute little lamps. Our heroes did not have much further to climb than just above the level of the big fence that surrounded the house, but to a rabbit that was pretty close to Everest.

After about an hour, the rabbits had travelled about ten feet. Because of the denseness of the foliage, they had lost sight of the crew on the ground, though they could still hear their encouraging cries. They paused for a rest, all breathing hard. "Didn't realise it'd be so tough," gasped Yank. Mac took a deep breath. "Not too far now, boys," he said through gritted teeth. "Come on Pongo! Nearly there."

Pongo was making particularly heavy weather of it, being fatter than the other two, and a good bit older as well, as he'd lied about his age so he could join the squad. His face was chalky white and his breath was coming in short sore gasps. They climbed on, then came to another halt, Pongo labouring up behind them. They had hit a problem they hadn't thought of. The branches were so thick that they now couldn't even see what height they were at, never mind get a clear shot with a catapult. "We're going to have to get along a branch," Mac said. "No sweat," said Yank, "I'll do it."

Yank picked up one of the thicker horizontal branches and stamped his feet on it a couple of times to make sure it was safe. Then he began to slowly edge along it. "Careful," warned Mac. "Hey, you look after yourself!" shouted Yank as he disappeared behind thick foliage. Pongo came up at last to the branch below Mac and slumped down in the crook of two strong twigs for a rest. "Chin up," said Mac.

There was a shout from their right. "Hey, daylight. Yay! I think we're high enough." Mac began to inch along the branch, placing his feet square on the wood, and using the tree above as a handrail. As the leaves thinned, the last of the day's sunlight span dizzily through the trees, casting strange and dizzy shadows everywhere. Mac shuffled patiently along, so concentrating on where he was putting his feet that he didn't notice that the string had unravelled from his wrist and was beginning to unwind from his waist and trail behind him.

Mac kept staring ahead, willing Yank to appear. At last he saw his friend whose smile turned suddenly to a look of alarm. "Mac, watch out for the string!" Just at that point Mac's foot rolled on the loose string and he lost balance. He fell and only just grabbed the branch with his paws, but the string was gone, drifting slowly to a smaller branch below where it hung in loops. Yank moved closer and grabbed his paw. "The string!" cried Mac, "What about the string?" They both looked down. It was beginning to unwind again, dropping slowly down. "Without the string," whispered Yank, "we're history."

Then, out of the corner of their eyes, they saw a large figure shuffling along towards it. "Pongo!" yelled Mac, "You'll never make it. It's too thin!" Pongo looked up and the two rabbits saw him blink. "Never did a brave thing before, sir," they heard him say gruffly. They watched in horror as he went, the wood vibrating and beginning to splinter beneath his big back paws. "Wait," cried Yank, "It's going to go!"

Pongo saw what was happening, then made a sudden heavy but agile movement towards the string. Pongo grabbed the end and was somehow able to propel himself up just as the branch gave way beneath him. He hung for a moment, twisting in space. Mac lunged down and briefly felt Pongo's paw, but it slipped through his grasp leaving only the end of the string. They saw Pongo fall, as if in slow motion, back through the branches. He seemed to be smiling up at them as he disappeared. Mac gulped, blinking back the tears. He felt Yank's paw on his shoulder. "C'mon Mac, you can't help him now. He's bought it." Mac shuffled to his feet. Suddenly he felt so guilty. "What have I done?" "Mac," said Yank gently, "You gave him - us all - something worth living for. Let's just make sure he didn't die for nothing."

Mac wound up the string. His paws were shaking. Then he inched back along the branch and looked through the leaves. They were about five or six feet higher than the level of the fence nearest to them. "That'll do," said Yank. Mac nodded. Tying the string securely to his wrist, he threw the coil down. After a while he felt a tug on the end of the line. The two rabbits, their other arms hooked carefully round a stout branch, pulled up the string and untied the coat hangers fastened to the end. Yank held onto them while Mac repeated the process, until the catapult had been sent up, then the string itself with a stone tied securely on the end, fastened in the exact way that Mac had taught Brains, and Sasha had taught Mac in a home that seemed a million miles away. "So far so good," he heard Yank mutter.

Right, thought Mac. He drew himself up to his full height and took the catapult, while Yank was tying the free end of the string onto a branch. The elastic of the catapult seemed incredibly tough. He'd practised a few times on the ground and had fired a good length but that had been on the ground and not half way up a fir tree with the fate of the universe, and the lives of the most gallant band of rabbits since ancient times, hanging on his every action. Yank held him round the waist. Steady, thought Mac, and he imagined the ancient rabbits with their blue painted faces sitting grimly watching the Romans wade ashore, knowing that there was going to be some fight but they were just the rabbits for it.

He drew the elastic back as far as he could, aiming at a point in the distance where he thought Fern and Windy would be, guided by the low line of the opposite fence which he could just make out in the growing dark. Hold, he thought, hold. Then he fired. "Go go go!" yelled Yank, and they watched anxiously as the string looped forward, then fell terribly short, not even half way up the garden. Yank breathed out. "Hard luck, Mac." They pulled the string back, then tried again, this time with Yank at the catapult. Again the stone fell short. They wound it back, and the string caught, tight, somewhere they couldn't make out. Mac gave a tug, then a larger one and the string came back, but without the stone. They stood in shocked silence. "We'll have to try again tomorrow," said Yank at last. Mac shook his head. He knew that this was their only chance, and they'd blown it. There would be no more tries tomorrow.

"IS THAT IT, THEN?" said a loud and squeaky voice in his ear. "What a STUPID game!" Mac whirled round, nearly toppling off the tree as he did so. A large black bird was perched on a branch right next to his head. "I mean," said the jackdaw, "I was standing here and I hear a noise like a TRIBE of ELEPHANTS coming up the tree and I saw the pair of you and I thought THAT'S something you don't see every day, two rabbits up a tree, this MUST be something good, or AT THE VERY LEAST one of them is going to have a heart attack, so that'll be funny, and though I have LOADS OF PEOPLE to see and things to do I'd stick around and ..."

"Listen, featherbrain," interrupted Yank, "This isn't a game. It's deadly serious." The jackdaw giggled, a noise deep in its throat. "Two RABBITS, two COAT HANGERS and a PIECE OF STRING? And it's SERIOUS? Well please excuse me, here's me thinking it's a complete JOKE. I MEAN I've not read in the NATIONAL GEOGRAPHIC recently about

RABBITS nesting in PINE TREES using COATHANGERS. I mean, is it the latest fad? Does DAVID ATTENBOROUGH know?"

Mac just stopped Yank knocking the bird off her perch. "Listen," he snapped angrily, "You might be too stupid to realise it but we've just lost one of our ..."

"HEY, do I know you?" said the jackdaw?

Mac snorted, "No, and as I was saying ..."

"YES, I know you. You were in the WOODS the other day when that GEEK tried to kill me. Is that the same catapult? Yes - YOU faced him down, didn't you? Yes, I'd know you anywhere. Big ears, whiskers and ugly teeth. It WAS you."

Mac nodded, "Yes, it was me. But ..."

"WOW," said the bird, "You're my HERO. Hey, do you know what this MEANS? According to the Jackdaw Law I have to do you three FAVOURS. What a DRAG!" It scratched the back of its head with a foot.

"Well, why don't you just go away?" said Mac.

The jackdaw thought about this for a moment. "Yeah, but then I'd still owe you two favours and I wouldn't be able to SLEEP properly till I'd done them and I don't imagine you pair go mountaineering EVERY DAY, do you? So I'd have the problem of FINDING YOU and the whole thing would just end up being a total BUMMER."

"Do us a favour and shut your cakehole," snapped Yank.

"Wait a minute," said Mac. "Yes" - he thought a little - "you could take the string and fly over that fence for us, couldn't you?" The rabbits were smiling again and slapping each other on the back. Yank punched the air. "Yeah," he said, "brilliant thinking, Mac." They turned to the jackdaw.

"So as a first favour," said Mac, "You could take this string and fly to that bit of the fence over there." He pointed out to the darkness.

"No," said the jackdaw huffily. "What?" cried Mac and Yank. "You promised us three favours!" "As I RECALL," said the jackdaw sarcastically, "Your first favour was for me to SHUT MY CAKEHOLE. So do you want me to talk now?" The rabbits nodded. "Well, that's TWO FAVOURS ALREADY," said the jackdaw.

"Why don't you wise up?" said Yank, "and stop ..."

"That'll be your third, then," said the jackdaw with satisfaction.

"Listen," said Mac angrily, "I saved your life because it was wrong for that boy to kill you just for fun."

"Though it might have been a blessing," muttered Yank.

"And what we're trying to do here is save a pig who might be going to die because it's not looked after properly and is shut up in a shed, and we're doing this not for a joke or a laugh but because it's right to help each other, just the same way as it was right to help you."

The jackdaw thought for a moment. "OK," it said at last, "What do I have to do?"

"So," said the jackdaw a few minutes later, still spluttering, "Let me get this right. You, TWO RABBITS UP A TREE, want me to fly with a piece of STRING to a DEER, in order that you can save a PIG?" The rabbits nodded. "Oh my GOD," said the jackdaw. "No-one's EVER going to believe this." The bird took off, keeping, with some difficulty as it was laughing so much, the string in its beak.

44

After a while the string stopped unwinding, then after a moment more, it went tense as it was tied into place. Yank tested it. "Secure," he said. "Secure," said Mac. "SECURE," said the jackdaw, who had just flown back and landed beside Mac. "Though the DEER was a bit shocked to see me. What happens next? Don't tell me. You …"

Mac and Yank fixed the coat hangers onto the string by the hooks. "Locked," said Mac. "Locked," said Yank. "LOCKED UP!" chuckled the jackdaw, "You should be LOCKED UP," and it flew off into the gloom, to tell its friends before it forgot.

"Here we go," said Mac.

"Into the wide blue yonder," said Yank.

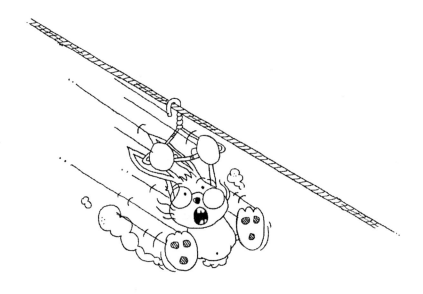

Mac took a run along the branch, holding onto the wide part of the hanger. He sagged as he left it and he half expected to plunge to earth like poor old Pongo, but the rope held, he tucked his feet up, and he soon found himself sliding down, picking up speed as the earth raced towards him. He had no real idea when to let go, but he trusted to luck, and when his stomach told him he'd not far to go, he jumped. There was a second's wait and then he hit the grass, rolling over and over. A thump behind him told him that Yank had landed too, somewhat further back. He squatted down, tried to get his breath back, and set his whiskers to the wind. Straining his eyes, he could make out the outline of the kennel, off to his right. He sensed movement inside. There was a great sweating, heavy scent, full of danger.

The dog was waking up. It, too, could feel something wrong. Mac moved off fast towards the kennel. The dog had begun a low, half sleepy growl. As Mac raced closer he could see the shape inside. Steam was rising. The dog was shifting, turning round, and Mac could see the gleam of its teeth. Mac was only inches away but the beast was shaking itself awake as it moved, and opening its eyes which were narrow and yellow. Suddenly it howled, a terrible and terrifying sound like a wolf, and took a pace forward. So this was it, thought Mac. He came to a halt right in front of the kennel. The dog fixed his eyes on Mac, and seemed to lick his lips. Mac froze, couldn't move a muscle. Just then, just as he could almost feel the teeth on his neck, Mac saw Yank hurtling in from the side, catching the kennel door full with his shoulder. The door flew back and hit the dog on the nose. It yelped in surprise and took a step back and Yank flung himself against the door. "Quick!" screamed Yank, as the dog began to move again. Mac jumped forward and shoved.

The door was forced shut for a second and Mac, before the dog could recover, fumbled, found the bolt and forced it home. They threw themselves back onto the grass, panting. The dog had begun to bark.

"Ow," moaned Yank. "What's wrong?" asked Mac anxiously. "Hit the door too hard," said Yank, "Burst my shoulder."

"You'll need to go back," said Mac, "Get a rest. I'll get the pig." Yank tried to argue but he was in a lot of pain. Mac took him back towards the fence. "Here," hissed Fern, whose night sight was good. "Over here!"

Mac watched his friend limp off towards the escape burrow, then turned. He looked back towards the house. It was still dark. He wondered when the man would realise there was no free pizza and turn up with his gun. He made a promise to himself that when he went home, if he went home, he would stay happy in his burrow and not have another adventure till the next book.

Moving to his right, towards where he knew the shed was, he eventually saw the low squat walls and went towards them. The shed was cold, clammy and stank, even from the outside. He shuddered to think of the condition of the animal inside. He found a door, and a latch. He lifted it and went inside, holding his nose against the smell. Perhaps the poor creature was already dead. "Shanghai," he whispered. "Shanghai!" A shape shifted, then moved unsteadily towards him. "Shanghai," said Mac, "I'm here to save your life."

"Oh, thank God," said a voice. "You must be a hairdresser."

Chapter 7

'TROUBLE JUST BEGINNING
TWO RABBITS DOWN BUT MAC'S
STILL SWINGING.'
(from 'The Battle of Shanghai')

The moon broke between clouds and Mac was able to see more clearly. What he saw was quite the ugliest creature he'd ever met.

"Shanghai?" he repeated.

The pig raised its eyes to heaven. "Lapsang Suchong out of Verdigris," it sighed. "I'm a pedigree, you know."

"Doesn't matter," said Mac. "We've got no time to spare. Come on."

Shanghai tottered forward and had a look out the door. He wrinkled his nose. "But my dear," he said, "The weather is absolutely ghastly. Why on earth would I want to go out there?"

"I'm rescuing you," said Mac, getting confused about the turn things were taking.

"Oh, how exciting," said Shanghai. "What from?"

Mac blinked. "You're getting badly treated," he said.

"Badly treated?" said Shanghai. "*Moi?* I must admit to being a little hungry and undergroomed recently, but I am waiting for my owner to come back and take me to his house in Kensington. I am to be introduced to society."

"You've been abandoned," said Mac. The pig looked at him then, with the air of someone speaking to an idiot, said, "Listen, I" - he pointed to himself with a trotter - "am a hugely expensive fashion accessory. You" - he waved his trotter towards Mac - "unless I am very much mistaken, are a … bunnyrabbit. We move in different circles, my dear. It would never work."

The pig tried to lever the door shut with his feet. "Now, if you'll excuse me …" Mac pushed back with his shoulder and thought fast. "It's true," he said, "but there are so many creatures who want to see you." The pig stopped shoving. "Are there?" he asked eagerly. "Oh yes," replied Mac, "You have lots of fans out there. They sent me to get you."

"Ah," Shanghai thought for a moment. "I always did want to go on tour. I suppose the arrangements would be suitable?" The pig was looking at itself in a broken piece of glass and turned to the side to get a better view. Mac nodded. "Oh, well, then. One must do what one must do to keep one's public happy." Shanghai staggered out into the open, Mac at his side.

"Oh, dear," said Shanghai. "My legs … would transport be laid on?"

"Yes," said Mac. "First stage by boat."

"How delightful," said Shanghai. "I hope there is a sun deck."

It took Mac quite a while to take the pig to the pond. Two things were clear. One was that Shanghai was in a bad condition. The other was that he was too stupid to realise it. They walked for some time, Mac whispering into the dark, "Skipper!" In the background, the dog was still barking. "Skipper!"

"Yes, please," said Shanghai dreamily, "lightly grilled with a little lemon juice."

"Mac!" They went towards the noise and Mac saw with joy the figures of Skipper and Dandy holding the table leg as it floated at the end of the pond. "Odd craft," murmured Shanghai. "It's the latest thing, sir," said Skipper. "Roll-on, roll-off. Very versatile."

"Yes," agreed Dandy, "You can even eat your dinner off it."

After a great deal of pushing and pulling they managed to get the pig on board and Mac watched them set off, the table twirling clumsily round as the two rabbits paddled. "See you on the other side," shouted Mac. "Toodle-oo," cried the pig. "Would you have my luggage sent on?"

51

Mac retraced his steps, eventually stumbling across the string, and followed it back. He was so tired he could hardly put one paw in front of the other. "You made it!" squealed Fern in delight when she saw him. Mac scrambled through the tunnel and was reunited with the others. Yank looked pale-faced but happy. "Everything OK?" Mac wearily gave the thumbs-up, as best he could, with a paw with no thumbs.

They trudged off back round the fence. Near the wood, a small patrol of the younger rabbits met them, and mobbed them, jumping up and down. "Pig arrived, sir," squeaked one of them. They walked the last yards in silence. Mac could see a larger group waiting and could hear Shanghai saying in a loud and irate voice, "No look here, I clearly asked for a herring." Fern looked quizzically at Mac. "It's a designer pig," said Mac. "It thinks it's a film star."

The waiting rabbits had formed two lines and as the others came in they cheered and waved their paws. The community was in a state of high excitement. At the clearing they met Brains, Skipper, and the rest of the Rabbit Response Force. They hugged and a few tears were shed. Yank went away to have his shoulder looked at.

"They're bedding the pig down for the night," said Brains. "It's eaten everything in sight and is still complaining."

"Great victory, sir," said Sparks. Brains nodded. "Yes, Mac, we've really proved something today, to ourselves more than anybody."

"And it's all down to you," said Windy.

Mac shook his head. He couldn't get the sight of Pongo's face out of his mind. He choked with tears. "Pongo," he said, "Pongo".

The crowd parted. "Oh, don't worry about me, sir. Take more than a few broken ribs and a major head injury to stop me." Mac couldn't believe his eyes. There was Pongo, his head wrapped in bloody bandages and balancing on a stick, but beaming all over his face. There was a pretty rabbit arm-in-arm with him. Mac was speechless. "To the victor the spoils," said Pongo.

Mac reached down and found his notebook.

VP (VICTORY PIG) NIGHT,

he wrote in big letters. ALL SAFE. TOTAL MIRACLE.

He began to laugh. Now the celebrations could begin.

Chapter 8

'WHAT'S A RABBIT TO DO
WHEN THERE'S NOTHIN' MORE
TO PROVE?
IS IT OVER?'
(from 'Mac's Darkest Day' by Rabbit Rage)

The friends stayed for a few days more in the wood, recovering from their adventures. Mac would like to have stayed but he knew he had a job still to do - to make sure his friend Fern and the pig Shanghai found a place of warmth and safety. He was worried about both of them. Fern was still very young and homesick and Shanghai, despite his huge appetite, had the look of an animal who needed some medical help. Also, although the rabbits in the wood were very friendly and would always have a very special place in Mac's heart, he couldn't keep living off them - they had enough food for themselves, but not a lot to spare. Mac knew how difficult it could be to feed a big family of rabbits even when you didn't have a Vietnamese pot bellied pig scoffing everything it could see. "I understand," Yank had said when Mac had told him he had to leave. "But where are you going to go?"

This was a question that Mac had asked himself. When he set off on this adventure he hadn't realised that he would end up caring for other animals, but perhaps that *was* the adventure. And adventures, Mac knew, had a beginning, a middle and an end. Mac had an idea that they had been through the middle bit and were now looking for a good end. All rabbits think they are geniuses, but they are also superstitious. You never see a rabbit walking under a ladder, or opening an umbrella indoors. They are great believers in luck. So Mac prepared to leave, even though he had no real idea where he

The day they left, all the rabbits waved goodbye. The girl he had called "Never" cried, though she was happy in a way, too, because she'd learned what a lot of humans don't know - that animals have personalities and feelings every bit

as important and real as people's. And the girl, for as long as she remembered this, would have her friends in the wood, and would always have the company of animals - which is a huge and great gift.

Mac and Fern and Shanghai trudged through the trees and into the open countryside, the farewells of theothers ringing in their ears. "Come back soon, Mac," Yank had said. "Things just won't be the same round here," and Pongo had presented Mac with a medal - I think it was a milk bottle top with a piece of coloured wool, with the words FOR BRAVRY written on it by the little girl in red crayon.

"How very dreary," Shanghai said, as they walked, "and how typical for there to be no public transport when you need it. How far did you say it was to the theatre?" But even Shanghai lapsed into silence as they walked on. Occasionally they would stop and forage for food but they didn't seem to get closer to anywhere, and the sheep they tried to talk to just stared at them and kept chewing in an insolent manner.

This is not the time to talk about sheep who deserve - and probably have - a book of their own. There is a great misunderstanding about sheep. All humans and most animals think sheep are stupid, but the truth is they belong to a gigantic secret society called the Fleecemasons, with their own secret language and ceremonies. All sheep are taught the secrets of Fleecemasonry at an early age and that is why suddenly they stop jumping about and doing cute and clever things and become really grave and serious. When they seem to be standing, chewing and being stupid, they are in fact thinking about the wisdom and secrets of the universe.

It is common knowledge that sheep have split the atom, and that there are at least three who have perfected space travel using anti-matter, but they are, of course, sworn to secrecy and can't tell anyone else, even other sheep.

So it is no wonder that Mac and Fern and Shanghai didn't get any help or advice from sheep. "Dull creatures," sighed Shanghai. The pig put a trotter to its stomach which was rumbling. "Isn't it time for afternoon tea?"

The animals spent two uncomfortable nights in the open during their walk. Mac was worried about both, but especially brave little Fern who had become really pale and silent. Animals have a way, sometimes, of giving up when they are depressed and ill. Mac desperately tried to cheer her up, recalling their great deeds of the past days, but she only became more withdrawn and quiet. Mac had another worry, and that was that they were being followed. On a few separate occasions, Mac had heard noises behind them, sniffed the air and sensed humans. He remembered the frightening time they'd had in the wood with the humans who had been trying to shoot Fern. They were obviously out to get her again. Fern didn't seem to care. Her eyes had become dull, her fur thick and matted. Shanghai only smelled food. VERY BAD wrote Mac in his book. He'd reached the last page.

On the fourth day after leaving the other rabbits, they were ambushed. As they stopped beside a track for Shanghai to eat some berries, two humans suddenly came out of the undergrowth and tried to grab them. Fern bolted and jumped a dyke into some trees, but Shanghai was caught. Mac watched helplessly as he was taken away. "Thank goodness," were the last words Mac heard him say. "Were you sent by my agent?"

Mac wandered for a long time. He, too, had lost all appetite. Everything he'd set out to do had ended badly. His friends were gone, or lost. He could see no signs of Fern, though he found a part of the wood which smelled strongly of her. The grass was beaten and there were a lot of broken twigs.

The humans must have got her, too. He couldn't go back to the other rabbits and tell them what a failure he was. Instead he just walked on until, one day, he came over a hill and there was the sea, lying flat and grey and huge. He had never seen anything so big. It filled him with amazement and broke his heart at the same time. He would never cross the sea as his heroic ancestors the explorer rabbits had done. Mac walked along the shore, sniffing the sea breeze, the salt on his whiskers, and after that sat down and probably would have died curled up under some grass, if it hadn't been for the owl.

Chapter 9

'SMELL OF DEATH
SMELL OF FEAR
IS RABBIT HEAVEN GETTIN' NEAR?'
(from 'Mac's Darkest Day')

The owl had come to Mac in his sleep, or maybe, he thought later, in a dream. Whichever it was, Mac had seemed to wake up and found this huge-headed bird standing over him. Strangely, he didn't feel afraid, even though owls are enemies of rabbits, and eat them if they are young enough. The owl was very old, grey feathered. It reminded him, for some reason, of Sasha. The owl didn't say very much but every word Mac remembered and later wrote down. Mac didn't understand what the owl said but seemed to understand, in a way he couldn't explain, what the owl *meant*.

All things, said the owl, *are as they always were.*

All rivers run to the sea.
Life is no more or less to me
Than a rabbit's whisker.
We rise, we fall
Like leaves and rise again and all
We do and say and gather
Is as important as a rabbit's whisker.

Mac had cuddled down and begun to drift away, across the ocean to a land where he could see, in his mind, a great throng of rabbits, even ancient rabbits with their blue faces. But the owl wasn't finished.

Mac, it said,
Go down once more to the shore.

Mac had done so, half in a trance, even forgetting his precious little bundle of possessions he'd carried all the way from home. As he stumbled on the sand, he hadn't even heard the humans behind him, and as they grabbed him, he fell at last asleep.

*It's at this point that everyone's meant to be weeping and wailing and tearing their clothes and shouting 'Bring Back Mac!' and swearing at the writer for ending the story in such a heartless manner. This is one of the great joys of being a storyteller, being able to bug people by making them sad, or cheer them up just when they feel it couldn't get worse. If this had been an ordinary story, I could do absolutely anything now. I could have Mac swallowed by a gigantic sea-serpent, or saved by a crack troupe of sheep armed with stun grenades. But this is not an ordinary story. It is Mac the Rabbit's story, and I copied it down after many hours of phone calls to him. You see, this is a **true story** and that's what makes it different.*

When Mac woke up it was a sunny afternoon. He was in a little hutch, nicely furnished and very comfortable. He had a small hot water bottle under the woollen blanket he was sleeping on. There was a dish of water and some nice fresh vegetables. Even more strangely, his little bundle was hanging on a peg by the door. On the wall, someone had pinned up his medal, and a Get Well Soon card. In spite of all this, he was unhappy. For the first time in his life he was imprisoned! He hopped up to the wire mesh and looked through. He was in what appeared to have been a farm. There were other buildings, and other wooden huts like his own. It was obviously a prison camp. He surveyed the scene grimly. There wasn't a cooler that could hold him, not Mac the Rabbit. He leaned on the mesh. Unexpectedly the door fell open and he fell out. He brushed himself down and turned round to survey the scene. His jaw dropped.

He was standing in a wide courtyard and everywhere he looked he saw scores of animals wandering about: dogs, geese, ducks, chickens. In fields beyond, there were horses, cattle and a little group of sheep. They all seemed happy, they all looked healthy. Even more amazingly, there were humans moving about too, chatting to them. And most strange of all, there was a little girl who looked exactly like Never. "Mac," she shouted with delight, "You're better!" Mac sidled up to her. "What's the story here?" he whispered.

The little girl told him the whole story. How she'd realised, after they'd left, that the three animals would need help, how she'd worried about them, how a kind woman came to her school and told them about this place, this animal centre where animals who needed help or were down on their luck could come and let humans look after them for a while. And how the little girl had stayed behind and told the woman Mac's story, then how they'd tried and failed to catch them and then finally succeeded, just in time. "Them?" asked Mac, and just at that moment he felt a nudge on the head and turned round to be greeted by Fern!

Fern looked slick and tall and healthy. After they'd hugged each other and shouted and cried a bit, Fern and Morgan took Mac on a tour of Mossburn Animal Centre. Mac had never seen so many animals, even ones he didn't know existed like lizards and racoons. They stopped at last outside a long shed. Fern pointed and Mac looked in the door. There were a group of pigs, knitting, and in the middle a large Vietnamese pot bellied pig was saying, "I think that was '96 in the Adelphi … I remember Derek Jacobi played my butler …" Mac quickly withdrew, laughing. They walked on till he was tired. "So it's not a prison camp, then?" "Nope," said Fern. "You're free to escape whenever you like." She pointed to the gate. "If it's just the same to you," yawned Mac, opening the door of his new house and reaching for his notepad, "I'll escape some other day."